Sasquatch

Written by Kelly Steele
Illustrated by Sarah Johnson

Copyright © 2018 All Rights Reserved
ISBN Number: 9781891423475
Library of Congress: 2018910600

Publishing

Jared was laying in his sleeping bag in the bed of the old 1977 GMC pickup. A cheap camper shell was his only protection.

Jared was scared, "Did you hear that?" He asked his brother Steve. "Hear what?" Steve replied. "I thought I heard a Sasquatch." "I only hear the creek, go back to sleep," replied his older brother.

Jared and Steve were on vacation with their parents. Their dad had pulled the truck off the road next to a large river in the Cascade Mountains of Washington State.

They had decided to camp here for the night. Jared and Steve were in sleeping bags in the bed of the truck. Their parents were in a tent by the mighty river.

The wind was blowing, rocking the truck back and forth. All at once Jared screamed, "We're going to die!"

The howl was as 100 wolves at the same time, the growl was as 50 grizzlies tearing apart the earth. The truck rocked violently side to side.

Jared screamed again, "Steve, wake up, Sasquatch has us!" Steve didn't wake up. The truck rose from the ground then slammed back down. The truck started sliding towards the river.

"Sasquatch is going to kill us!" screamed Jared. Yet Steve slept on. As the wind howled and the truck rocked, Jared looked out the window of the camper shell.

There stood a big foot staring him right in the eye. Big foot had pushed the truck right up to the edge of the river.

The Sasquatch howled in fury as he lifted the truck and tossed it over the rocks and into the current.

The truck was floating down the middle of the river, yet Steve slept on.

Then it happened, the truck went over a 50 foot waterfall. Upon hitting the bottom, the camper shell flew from the truck.

Jared looked over the bed rails of the still floating truck. He screamed in terror as anather Sasquatch reached into the bed of the truck and plucked him out.

"Steve, Steve!" he screamed as he kicked and fought, trying to get away from the Sasquatch.

Jared had heard many stories of a band of Sasquatches who lived in the cascades of Diablo, Washington. He was terrified on this vacation, and now the Sasquatches had him.

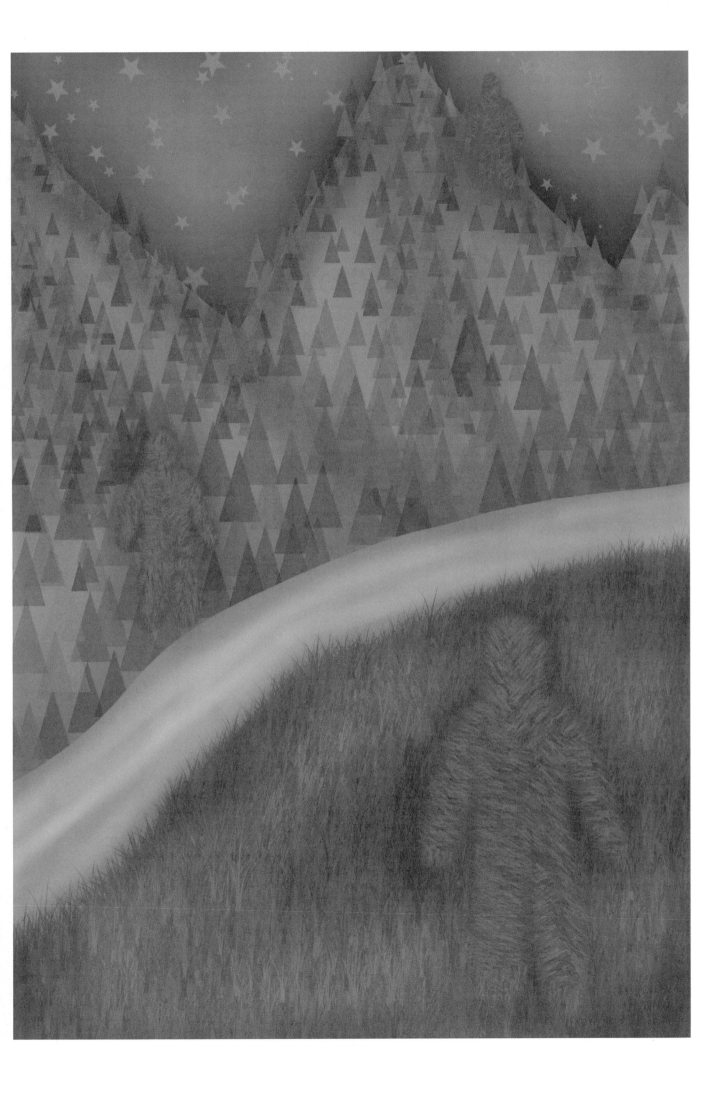

As Jared fought and fought trying to escape the Sasquatches hold on him, he awoke.

The sun was peeking through the large pine trees in the East. Jared was covered in sweat and tangled in his sleeping bag. Steve was asleep in his own sleeping bag at Jared's side.

After breakfast, cooked on a nice fire, the boys played down at the river's edge while their parents cleaned up camp and got ready to leave. A deafening roar went through camp.

Jared told his brother Steve about his nightmare. Steve laughed, "You are silly. There is no such thing as a Sasquatch." "Well if that is true, what do you call that?"

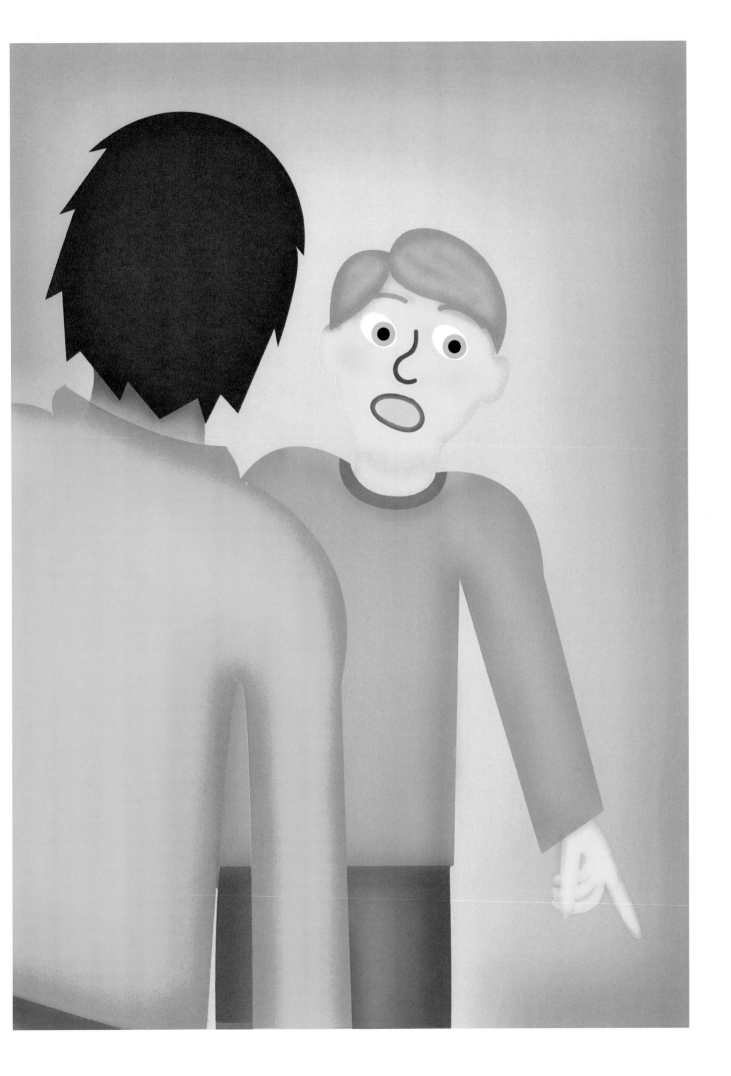

There in the mud by the shore of the river was a giant footprint, a Sasquatch foot print. The two brothers ran back to camp as fast as they could.

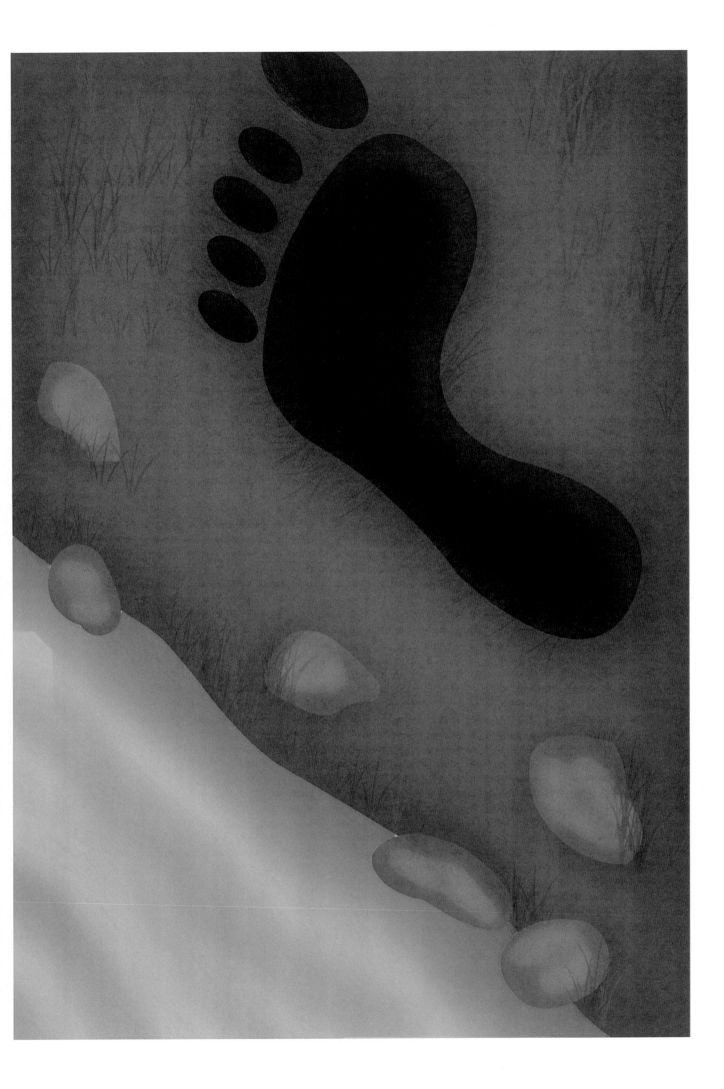

Their mother said, "Oh good, you boys are back, I was just going to call you. We are ready to go." "But Mom, Mom, a foot print, it's a big foot. Mom come look, it's by the river."

"Oh, you boys, always making up stories." "But Mom, it's real, come on Mom, come see." "Now you boys are just making up stories so that we will stay here longer. Now get in the truck."

"But Mom, it's true, Mom, come see." "You boys get in the truck and stop this big foot nonsense, I'll have your father tan your hides."

The boys dejectedly climbed into the cab of the truck and down the road they went. As they neared Seattle, Jared looked at Steve.

"No one will ever believe us!" he cried. "Maybe it's better if they don't," replied Steve. "Maybe we better forget about it Jared. Maybe it was all just a bad dream."

As Jared, Steve, Mom, and Dad rose to the top of the space needle, a blood curdling scream rose above the river in the Cascade town of Diablo.

The End

Ross the Rooster Takes A
Vacation

Ross The Rooster's
Halloween Fright

Ross The Rooster's First
Christmas

Ross The Rooster's Day
At The Fair

La Leyend A Del Lago
De Osos Bear Lake

Ross The Rooster Saves
Christmas

Ross The Rooster
Discovers Gold

Ross The Rooster Goes
Down Under

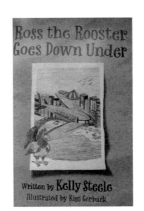

Bear Lake The Legend
Continues

Ross The Rooster And
The Gypsy Vanner

A Thanksgiving To
Remember

Ross The Rooster Goes
Camping

The Legend of Bear
Lake

Made in the USA
Las Vegas, NV
01 April 2022

46690920R00033